Pronunciation of names and words in the book.
*Please use this to learn the correct way to say names and words in the book.

Correct spelling:	Way to sound it out
Devyne	Divine
Philistine	Feel- a- stine
Doeg	Doe- ag
Goliath	Ga-lie-if
Judah	Ju-da
Samuel	Sam-u-el
Abner	Ab-ner
Bethlehem	Beth-la-ham
Ahimelch	A-him-e-lek
Edomite	E-do-might
Elah	E-la
Israel	Is-real

Commandment
#8 (Do not steal)

BIBLE TALES

On a gloomy, dark Saturday night, little Devyne waited up
late for another Sunday morning at his church. Every since
he could remember his parents always read him stories
from the bible and related them to the problems he was
facing. So being asked to clean the church this Sunday,
Devyne decided to make his cleaning into a great game of
treasure hunting. "There has to be something great in that
building said Devyne, "and if it's there I will find it!", he
quickly added. As he fell asleep his mom and dad woke
him up shortly a few hours later. Springing up fast, "good
morning mom", running off to the bathroom to brush his
teeth and to wash his face. "Devyne stop running around,
acting all crazy", his father added, "you still have an hour
or so before service". "You know that boy loves church",
his mother said to his dad. As they arrived at the building
the hope of finding something new made the service go by
quickly. "Devyne we will be back to get you in two hours",

his mother said. As the pastor gave all the boys their tasks and places to clean, Devyne interested to start, already planned to run to the basement and next to the attic, if he didn't find anything. For all the other kids cleaned out of hope of receiving something like candy or money, but Devyne knew there was a treasure in this place, he had to just, find it. Keeping watch over the time, he knew he only had a little under two hours, so into action he sped off. As he searched high and low through the basement, he found nothing but garbage and more garbage. All the little kids cleaning and not searching put Devyne at ease for he knew they would not unbury his treasure, but it awaited only him he felt inside. So Devyne continued his search harder and harder. "Junk, junk, junk and more junk", Devyne said loudly as he glanced at the time he saw he only had a little under an hour left. He searched the basement high and low, corner to corner finding nothing, but stacks of paper, old dusty paintings and broke down music equipment. Pressing the key on the old piano nothing happened, "this has to be the perfect place to hide a treasure",Devyne thought. "Why would they not throw it away?", he wondered looking the old piano over, top to bottom. As Devyne lifted it up, looking behind him, wanting no one to see him, a whirl wind of dust came from the inside and almost knocked him off of the piano stool. Coughing and spitting up, Devyne thought this is going to be harder than I thought. "It's time for the attic", Devyne said racing off. As he opened the attic door, he discovered by the look there was more junk in here than in the basement. "I better get started", Devyne said with a sigh. He searched and searched some more not seeing anything worth being called treasure. Time flew and as he glanced down shocked," five minutes!" said Devyne stunned. "I have to hurry up I know it's up here", Devyne said worried, wondering if he would find anything with time winding down. Through the church attic window he could see all the children parents pulling up. He kept searching with great speed until he heard the familiar sound of his father's horn, he used when he arrived some place. Devyne thought to himself, "of all the times, now my father decides to show up on time". But Devyne kept searching finding nothing until he glanced into a pile of dusty, dirty books and saw a strange book that sparkled and shined, and said, HOLY BIBLE",

across the front. Devyne said to himself," I've never saw a bible as beautiful as this". He decided, this would be his treasure. Tucking it away and hiding it, he ran down the stairs, finding his mom and dad waiting with the pastor, and all the other children and their parents gone. "Let's go", Devyne father said very calm, a little mad at the wait. Devyne hurried off into the car with a great smile, and his treasure tucked away. The whole way home brought such a rush of hope and interest to Devyne awaiting to see that great sparkle and shine again his treasure had. "Devyne, do you want to stop to get something to eat". "NO, that's alright!", he told his father. As they pulled in the drive way it felt as though they were still in motion, as Devyne jumped out and raced to the door, took out his house keys, unlocked the door, and ran inside leaving the door wide open for his parents. "What's wrong with that son of yours?", his father asked. "He probably has to use the bathroom", his mom answered back. As Devyne sped through the house, he reached his room and in such a rush he left his bedroom door wide open. He then took out the book and stared at it with great happiness and amazement. So caught up in the beauty of the book, Devyne didn't hear his parents come in the house and head toward his room. As they pushed open the door, Devyne tried to hide the book on the side of him. "What is that your hiding?, his mother asked. "Nothing mom", he answered back quickly.

"Well if it's nothing, you don't mind showing me and your father what nothing looks like". "Sssssssssssssss", Devyne said as he let out a great gasp of air, bringing the book to his lap. "That's a beautiful book", his mom said as his parents walked closer and sat down next to him. "Where did you get that from?", his mom asked. "Oh, I found it while cleaning out the church, in a pile of garbage", Devyne answered very fast, running out of breath. "Does the pastor know you have this?", his father asked. "Well I was going to tell him but you guys came, and it was in a pile of garbage so I didn't think he would mind", Devyne answered back. "So you know you will have to return this back to the church honey. This book looks like it cost too much for someone to just throw it away," his mom said still steering at it. At least can I look it over tonight and study it before we take it back?", Devyne pleaded hands to his chest almost begging. "Okay, but tomorrow we have to bring it back", his father said. "Open it up Devyne so we can all look at it together", his father added. As Devyne little finger rubbed over the glowing title his parents looked on with great wonder at the glow the book held. As Devyne stuck his little fingers almost a quarter of a way in the book, the pages seemed to glow inside, as it looked like it held the sun inside. Devyne slowly opened the book to 1st Samuel chapter17, the story of David and Goliath, the title said across the top of the book. But the wording wasn't like any other book Devyne or his parents ever saw as the wording seemed to come to life and glow with great radiance. "Here you read it", Devyne said to his mother. "It's your book", she said back. "Just feel the letters as you read and sound the words out". The words seemed to hold the attention of the whole family, as they all steered on, breaths lost also. As Devyne touched the title to sound it out, the words grew bright, and the book started to shake. First a little, enough that Devyne thought it was how nervous he was and then enough, to know it wasn't his nerves as the whole bed seemed to follow along almost knocking them all off.

And suddenly a burst of light came from within the book, and before anyone of them could move, sucked them all in, and closed on the bed behind them. Rubbing their heads they all looked up in a patch of grass, and noticed that they weren't in Devyne's room anymore. As his father stood up he noticed two large armies which covered the whole field standing in front of them positioned as if they were ready to fight. "Dad, do you think we are where I think we are?", Devyne asked. "Son, I don't know", his father answered back unsure. As time went on they noticed a young boy coming in their direction. As the boy came closer Devyne jumped up!"David, David, David! Yes I know who you are. Dad I was right, yes...yes...yes. I can't believe I am really meeting King David!". "King David", the boy said back. "I am not a King, just a simple sheep herder. Yes, my name is David and I am the son of Jesse, and how do you know my name?". "Because you are in the bible and this is the book of 1st Samuel", Devyne answered back sooo fast he almost lost his breath. "The book of Samuel, what do you mean?", David asked feeling lost. "Devyne be quiet", his father said. "He doesn't know what you mean", he added whispering into his sons ear. "Hello David, I am Dane, Devyne's father and this is Crystal his mother, and of course you have already met my big head son, Devyne", his father said laughing. Devyne father also asked, "David can you please tell me if this is gonna be a war between those two armies down there", he said pointing in the direction of the war. "No, that is Goliath, and his Philistine army, and that there on the other side, is the army of Israel, which my brothers are fighting for. But I am about to defeat mighty Goliath for he defies The Lord almighty and His army, also the King said that he will give a great deal of wealth to the man who kills him, and he will also give him his daughter in marriage, and free him and his father's family from paying taxes in all of Israel. Please wait here for me and I will return", said David walking away towards the battle lines. Devyne, his mother and father sat up in the grass and watched as David came closer to the other guys and they be-ginned to talk to each other. "Dad, you know David is going to beat Goliath, right?", Devyne asked. "Yes, Devyne but I don't care about that. My only concern is to find someone that can help us get back home". As they looked back up, David was walking closely again. As David came closer he looked angry at what was just said to him. "What happened?", asked Devyne almost upset, but curious. "My brothers got mad at me, because I want to fight Goliath". "David you have to fight him. You will beat him, trust me", Devyne said trying his hardest to persuade David. "Devyne be quiet", his father fired back. "David, we need your help. We need to find a church, a pastor, the king, or someone who will be able help us. We need to get home, and we don't know where to go or what to do". But before Devyne father could finish talking, the kings royal guards, came and asked with great authority and power, "Who is David?. For he is wanted by King Saul". "We also have to see the king", Devyne father said, as the king's servants acted quickly, drawing their swords and spoke, "no, only David". "Please wait calmly and I promise I will be back and I will help you find the right help you need, in order to get your family back home", David said as he calmly left following the kings servants. As they all laid there together thinking, they fell asleep waiting for David to return, for what seemed like hours. But there peaceful sleep was stopped from all the noise, as little Devyne rose and saw David walking closer to Goliath. "Wake up, wake up, it's about to happen", Devyne shouted. "What's about to happen?", his mother asked, getting up and rubbing her eyes. "David is about to beat Goliath", answered Devyne. As they watched in silence, Devyne took off running to get a closer look. "Come back here", shouted his parents chasing after him. About a football field up, Devyne stopped near some bushes in good sight and now also able to hear what was being said. As his parents reached him, they shouted, "Devyne you are on punishment forever when we get home", but again his father was interrupted by Goliaths loud shout. "Am I a dog, that you come at me with sticks?" Then angry, he spoke bad about David and his God. "Come here", he said, "and I'll give your flesh to the birds of the air and to the animals of the field". But David answered quickly back, without thinking, in boldness and in confidence, "You come against me with sword and spear, and javelin, but I come against you in the name of The Lord Almighty, The God of the armies of Israel, whom you have went against. This day The Lord will hand you over to me and I will beat you down and also cut your head off. Today I will give the bodies of the Philistine army to the birds of the air and the animals of the earth, and the whole world will know that there is a God in Israel. All those who come here will know that it is not by sword or spear that The Lord saves, but for the battle belongs to The Lord and He will give all of you into our hands". As the Philistine moved closer to fight David, David ran faster toward the battle line to meet him head on, at the same time reaching into his bag, and taking out a small stone.

With great speed and accuracy, he slung it, and it struck the mighty Philistine in the middle of his forehead. The stone flew faster and with more power than a missile and sank right into his forehead, and he fell face down on the ground. David won the battle over the Philistine, with a sling shot and a stone, and without a sword in his hand, he struck down the Philistine and killed him. David ran and stood over him, rejoicing in his victory through God. He took hold of the Philistines sword and took it out of its holder, and as he laid there, he cut off his head. When the Philistines saw that their hero was dead, they turned and ran. Then the men of Israel and Judah came forward and with a mighty shout ran after the Philistine army. As David stood there, Devyne sped off again running toward David. David seeing Devyne, walked toward him and they met each other with a big hug. "David I told you, you could do it. And I also know all the things that will follow this", Devyne said. As Devyne's mother and father finally caught up, hearing the last words out of Devyne's mouth, his father said angrily, " Devyne, I told you about running off. I am your father and you know better than to disobey me. "Sorry dad", Devyne said. "Matter of fact, let me speak to you over here", pointing to a tree a couple of feet away, " and honey can you please talk to David about us getting home". "Okay", his mother said. Walking away Devynes father spoke, "Devyne", he called to him. "Yes", Devyne answered. "Son, you can't tell David what's going to happen. He doesn't know because we are in his time, and if you help him you can change the course of history forever. Which will change the bible and also change the world and stop running and leaving us", his father calmly added also smiling. "I am very sorry dad, and I promise to do as you ask", Devyne said back sincerely. "Can you two boys come back and listen", Devynes mother said. As they came close David began talking, " your wife has told me that you are all from the future, and that you came here through a magical book". "The Bible", Devyne said very fast, shutting up just as quick, seeing the look his father gave him. David then finished, "I can bring you to the priest Samuel, and I believe that if anyone can help you it would be him". As Saul watched David and Devyne's family he said to Abner, commander of his army, "Abner, whose son is that young man?", speaking of Devyne. Abner replied, "as surely as you live, O king, I do not know". "And the people he is with", the king asked. "Them either", Abner answered. The king said, "find out whose son this young man and strong people are, and report back to me, immediately". While David and Devyne's family was speaking, Abner came close and took them and brought them before Saul. "Whose son are you, young man, and who are your friends?", Saul asked him. David said, "I am the son of your helper Jesse of Bethlehem, and yes, these are my friends, Dane, Crystal and their son Devyne", waving at the king. After David was finished talking with Saul, Johnathan, king Sauls son became one in spirit with David, and Devyne's family and he loved them just as they loved themselves. One night, sitting in David's room, Devyne and David sat awake and talked while everyone else in the Kings castle slept. "David, do you think me and my family will ever get back home?". "Yes, you will as soon as I am able to get some time to take your family to see the priest. I have been sooo busy with running Sauls army lately, but I promisc to gct you guys home. Devyne can you please tell me about where you are from?". "Well where I am from, there are no armies fighting in the open, and no kings". "No kings", said David very interested interrupting Devyne sitting on the edge of his seat. "Nope, no kings. Just a president, and young boys like me who go to school all day and learn, and then come home and we play all day". "What about your fathers sheep?". Devyne laughed, "my father has no sheep, he probably wouldn't even know what to do with sheep", Devyne said and both of them laughed together. "So how does your family eat?". "My father works by building houses and my mother designs and makes clothes, and I don't work. I play all day, running and riding my bike. I miss my home so much David, but I bet you would really like it. When we see the priest, you should come with us". "Maybe", said David falling asleep. Devyne sat there steering at his parents and David, sadly knowing he should of never took the book in the first place. It was in taking what didn't belong to him that had gotten him and his family into all of this trouble. Time passed and slowly but surely Devyne drifted off to sleep. Everyone awoke early from the loud cheer of the people screaming, "Saul has killed his thousands, and David his tens of thousands". But that day an evil spirit from God came upon Saul. As David was playing the harp, as he did usually when Saul didn't feel good, Saul had a spear in his hand and threw it, saying to himself, "I'll pin David to the wall and kill him and his friends". But David dodged him and his spears twice. Running back to his room out of breath, David opened the door and quickly slammed it back, putting the big wooden beam over the door to secure it.

Turning around out of breath he saw Devyne and his family looking at him scared wondering what was going on, now seeing the champion bent over breathing heavy and as scared as them. Finally David spoke, "Saul is crazy, and he wants to kill us, in fact he just tried to kill me twice". As he was speaking Johnathan came and knocked on the door, sending all of them into each other's arms, afraid it was the king and his men coming to finish the job. Hearing the knock again they knew it couldn't be the king and his men, because they would never knock, but wanting to get in, probably would have broken the door down. "Who is it?", David asked with little Devyne by his side. "It's Johnathan open up. I come in peace and to let you know what I have learned". Knowing the love Johnathan had for all of them, they quickly opened the door, and as Johnathan stood there, David snatched him in. Johnathan quickly told them of his father's plan to kill them tomorrow because of the fame David was getting, and Devyne and his family because he knew the love that David had for them. Devyne felt so bad inside for he knew it was really his fault, anyways for even touching the book. Now he was beginning to see why it was never a good idea to take things that didn't belong to you, no matter how dirty the place you found it in. So together they came up with a plan to leave when the sun rose. That night they all sat under the locked door and talked. "I have to get you guys out of here and home",

David said. David quickly said again, "Tomorrow it will all be over, for we will leave in the morning for we have to meet with Ahimelch the priest of Nob. And I know he will be able to help you guys get home as soon as we get there". "I thank you so much for all your help and concern", Devyne's mother said. "Well please get some rest, because I think tomorrow we will have to do a lot of running", said David. On that quiet night, hours passed calmly, holding a lot of problems for all of them for the next day. In the morning, Johnathan went out to the field for his meeting with Devyne's family. He had a small boy with him who was a part of their plan. David knew Johnathan would shoot three arrows in the air, then send the little boy to run and find the arrows with a message. Then Johnathan gave the boy his weapon and told him to carry them back to town. After the boy had gone, David and Devyne's family got up from the south side of the stone and bowed down before Johnathan three times, with their faces to the ground. These customs were not what Devyne and his family were used to but they kindly followed David's example and ways. Then they all kissed each other and cried, but David and Johnathan cried the most. Johnathan feeling it was time then told them to go in peace, for we have a sworn friendship with each other in the name of The Lord, saying " The Lord is a witness between you and me and between your children and mines forever". Then David and Devyne's family left, and Johnathan went back to the town. David and Devyne's family walked and walked for hours, and hours until it felt like they had walked for days. As they approached a town they saw a sign that said, "NOB". And they walked up to the building that looked like a church to see the priest Ahimelch. Ahimelch trembled when he met them and asked, "why are y'all alone, and no one of royalty is here You guys?". David answered back, "the king charged me with a special matter and said to me, that no one is to know anything about your mission and instructions. As for my men, I have told them to meet me at a special place. Now then what do you have at hand?". "Give me five loaves of bread, or whatever you can find", David said. The priest turned to David's friends and said, " what about them?". "Oh yeah, excuse me your royal priesthood this is Devyne and his family, they are from another place", said David. "Another place?", the priest said shocked. "Yes another place, the future actually they called it", David said. Continuing "they were sucked in by a magical book". "A magical book", the priest asked. "Yes, a magical book and King Saul is trying to kill us all. And the real reason we came to see you is they need to get back home before things get really crazy, and I knew you would be the only person to understand and help them. Also, I need any weapon that you may have in your possession, because we had to leave on a quick note and I couldn't bring anything", David said. Now one of Saul's servants was there that day, held before The Lord, he was Doeg the Edomite, Saul's head Shepard. David asked the priest, as a lightbulb went off in his head, "don't you have a spear or a sword here?. I really would feel more comfortable because once the King notices us gone he will come after us, and I need a weapon to protect us, for they aren't coming to talk with us". The priest replied, "the sword of Goliath's the Philistine whom you killed in the valley of Elah is here. It is wrapped in a cloth behind the robe over there", he said pointing, "and I also kept the spear which is sitting next to it. If you want it take it, there is no other weapons here but those two". David replied, "there is none like it, please give it to me".

As the priest went off to grab the bread, he began rumbling through a bunch of old books. "Excuse me sir, what do you plan to do about us?", asked Devyne. "I believe I have a book with a similar story in it", the priest returned, "but I always thought that it was a myth". As Devyne looked back he saw David holding the giant sword in great wonder. As the priest continually searched, no one noticed Doeg the King's servant sneak out the back door and quickly make his way back to the King's palace so that he could tell the King what he saw, knowing it would be worth great reward. Still searching the priest pulled out a small stepping ladder and reached up on top of the bookshelf, grabbing a book with a great amount of dust built up on top of it. "That book looks like it hasn't been used in years", said Devyne laughing. "Yes I know, it was given to me by my father, and has been in our family for a very long time. My father always told me to guard it well, for one day it would come in a great need and be really useful. And so I guarded it so well that I forgot where I placed it for a minute", said the priest returning with a laugh. "So you put it on a shelf?", asked Devyne. "Well, the best place always to hide something is right in plain view", said the priest. Well miles away, Doeg the Edomite just reached the Kings palace, and rushed up to the King to tell him about David and his strangely dressed friends. Doeg told the King everything, how they arrived at Nob, to see the priest for help, for food, weapons, and help getting his friends home. The King rewarded Doeg with money, and begun speaking to his army to get ready to go after David and his friends and to bring them back, including the priest who was so kindly willing to help them knowing they were enemies of the King. Back at Nob, everyone sat at the table looking at the book and enjoying the bread the priest baked. "Excuse me Doeg........Doeg", the priest called out loud. The priest got up and looked around for Doeg after not answering his call, and saw the back door completely open, and his horse gone also. Running back to the table the priest said out of breath, "we have to hurry up. I believe Doeg, Saul's helper has left to report to the King of your arrival here". "That's just what we needed", David added. As the priest flipped through the pages he began reading from a page outlined in gold writing, that shined like Devyne's book back at home, but just in a funny language. "Excuse me, but what does all of that mean?", asked Devyne still looking at the funny writing. Reading, the priest, "it means before the sun goes down, and the moon comes out, a portal will be opened and a gate, will appear that will carry you guys back home". Looking out the window the priest finished," and that's about less than an hour". "Well what about you and David, will you two come back with us?", asked Devyne sadly already knowing in his heart the answer to his question. "My job and duties are to the people here, and to leave would be to leave the people or abandon the purpose of The Lord, and I will never leave the people or my God", added the priest. David knelt down next to Devyne and hugged him and took off his robe, and placed it across Devynes shoulders. "I also have to stay", said David. "I have to watch over my family and try to see what the ending to this book you always talk about, The Bible". Smiling at Devyne to try to cheer him up knowing his words weren't what little Devyne expected to hear, he continued, "But I promise I will always remember you and your family, I promise". As David and Devyne began to hug, loud noises of horses racing could be heard coming in the distance. As Devyne's mother looked through the window, she could see a great number of soldiers on horses approaching. "Enough of the hugging", she quickly said, "or else no one is going to be going anywhere". The priest happened to look out the window and also saw that the sun beginning to set in the distance, he added, " a couple more minutes and then we can open up the book. Follow me this way". They all began to run towards the back and at that, they heard the noise of the horses stop and someone began banging hard on the door. They all continued to run through the house, towards the basement. This is a secret way through the town into the next town", added the priest. As they came closer to the light at the end of the tunnel, they heard hard, fast foot steps behind them. As they looked, they noticed the soldiers closely behind them. "You are my responsibility", said David. "The Lord protects me against everything that I have ever come against, and I know He will continue to lead me". With that said, David stopped and drew his sword in a fighting stance. As they continued to run, the priest very scared, feeling this was all going to end the wrong way, accidentally dropped the book.

As soon as the book hit the floor, it began to shake, and then out of nowhere and as quick as lightening, the book cast a light from within it, that shinned brightly, lighting up the whole tunnel. At first no one knew what was going on, but when the light sparked, it made everyone cover their eyes, but having his back turned to the book and their eyes in front, it gave David a great fighting advantage, that when they stopped to cover their eyes, and David continued to swing his sword. Knocking them one, two, at a time, he fought in a way the greatest warrior would be proud of, he kicked a blinded solider running full speed with all his might, sending him into more running forward. As they looked up, at the priest, he began to say, "this is the moment we all waited for. The time is here, you must leave now! All you have to do is jump in", the priest yelled, through all the noise. Scared, they all jumped when they heard the loud sound of metal being banged against metal. At that they noticed it was David, fighting Saul's troops alone, holding his own ground, as a fearless warrior would do. Not one nick, scratch or drop of sweat, David one handed grabbed a hand full of material and threw men, twice his size and weight, sword still in hand. At that, the book opened up. It opened up flat on it's back, and they knew that was what they had waited for the whole time, and all they had to do now, was to jump in with no hesitation. With that Devyne's mother said, "thank you so much," and she jumped in. Devyne's father shook the priest and yelled," thank you", so loud that his voice vibrated all the way to David still fighting. Knowing that even though David didn't answer, he knew in his heart that David felt his good bye and one of the reasons for his desire of fight now was for his family, and with that, he looked, at his son, and said, "say your goodbye son, and come on, will be waiting", and with that, followed his wife, and jumped in. Devyne looked greatly saddened as David fought, and with everything in him yelled over all the noise, "David I won't leave without you!", with tears streaming down his face. The priest stood there shocked, not knowing what to say at the saddened boy, but finding the words he said," look Devyne the light in the book is beginning to blink in and out as though the portal is about to close you have to leave now". David still fighting, but hearing what the priest said to Devyne, swung hard and knocked the two soldiers down to their feet, almost looking like a pile of leaves as hurt soldiers laid on top of others, and yelled, "Devyne, you need to leave now or else you will be stuck here with me forever". With tears in his eyes and his mind already made up, Devyne lifted his head up and replied, "then I am staying here with you". As the men David was fighting struggled and began to get back up, and more soldiers pushing to get pass to get into the fight from the top of the stairs. David yelled loudly and with the strength and power of God, knocked all of the men about 15 plus soldiers and their weapons to the floor, and with one quick movement, turned and said, "I love you", to Devyne and drew his spear from his side and threw it hard at Devyne. Seeing the spear fly at him with a speed that seemed to cut through the air, but come at him in slow motion, Devyne missed the spear, though so close it went through the corner of the robe, still jumping out the way, the light caught a piece of him, and sucked him into the book, screaming," NO, I WON'T LEAVE, I WON"T".

With the loud screaming, Devynes parents woke up next to Devyne shaking him, to wake up, telling him it was only just a bad dream. Devyne jumped up and hugged his mom, looking into her eyes, and into the eyes of his father, them looking into his, no one wanting to think the impossible, all knowing it really wasn't a dream at all. As they looked at their side, they noticed the book laying there partially covered up by Devynes blanket. As his mom and dad went to get up both rubbing their heads, Devyne looked and knew there was no way that he was going to make his parents believe that this was more than a bad dream. He sat there wishing he had proof, because it felt to real to be a dream, cutting off his thought, he smiled and said, "mom, do we really have to return the book tomorrow?". As she smiled at her only son, she also wondered was it possible for all of them to have the same dream, and all feel that strong about it, she just smiled, speechless. But caught up in her thoughts, she never answered him. As Devyne picked the book up and held it on his lap, rubbing the letters written across the top, 'HOLY BIBLE', a tear fell from his eye on top of the book. Feeling sad, he quietly told his parents sorry and told them he realized this was all his fault, for being disobedient, breaking the 8th commandment (thou shall not steal). His parents smiled and told him that they love him, still not sure what just happened. As they turned to leave, Devyne still with tears in his eyes looked on the floor, and sitting there on top of his dirty clothes sprawled out was a purple robe.. Devyne smiled hugging the book tight.....Knowing it wasn't a dream.

The End...

Moral:

In life, there is a reason things shouldn't be taken without asking. Things can be harmful to ourselves and to those we love. We also may not see the danger at the time because we are so caught up by the beauty it possesses. If we ask we learn the importance and in the end it might even be given to us. But there also may be a reason something is put up, that you don't know why or need to know. So never steal, this was given and commanded of us for a specific reason, from God himself. And we should obey.

Made in the USA
Middletown, DE
10 September 2018